SNOWMEN
AT HALLOWEEN

Caralyn Buehner

pictures by

Mark Buehner

Dial Books for Young Readers

One autumn day the air turned
cold and it began to snow.
We went outside and made some
snowmen standing in a row.

My sister had a box of dress-ups
out for Halloween,
And soon all those snowmen were
the scariest we'd ever seen!

We went off to a party, and trick-or-treating too,
Then headed home in the dark when everything was through.

As we passed our snowmen, I thought I saw one wink.
Did they want to have fun too? Well, this is what I think:

It's a dark and spooky night, but the snowmen aren't afraid—
They'll follow one another in a Halloween parade,

Gliding down the moonlit streets into the village square,
Beckoned by the twinkling lights and lanterns hanging there.

They'll see lots of orange pumpkins heaped up in a pile.
Every snowman gets to carve a very scary smile.

They'll like playing all the games,
and "fishing" for a prize,
And have their faces painted
by an artist in disguise.

Some bite into caramel treats,
which give them gooey grins;
Others bob for apples in the
apple-bobbing bins.

For a coin the fortune teller sees a snowman's fate.
Will it be warm sun or snowstorms they'll anticipate?

Maybe they will wander through a maze made out of hay.

Twisting turns and dead ends make it fun to find the way.

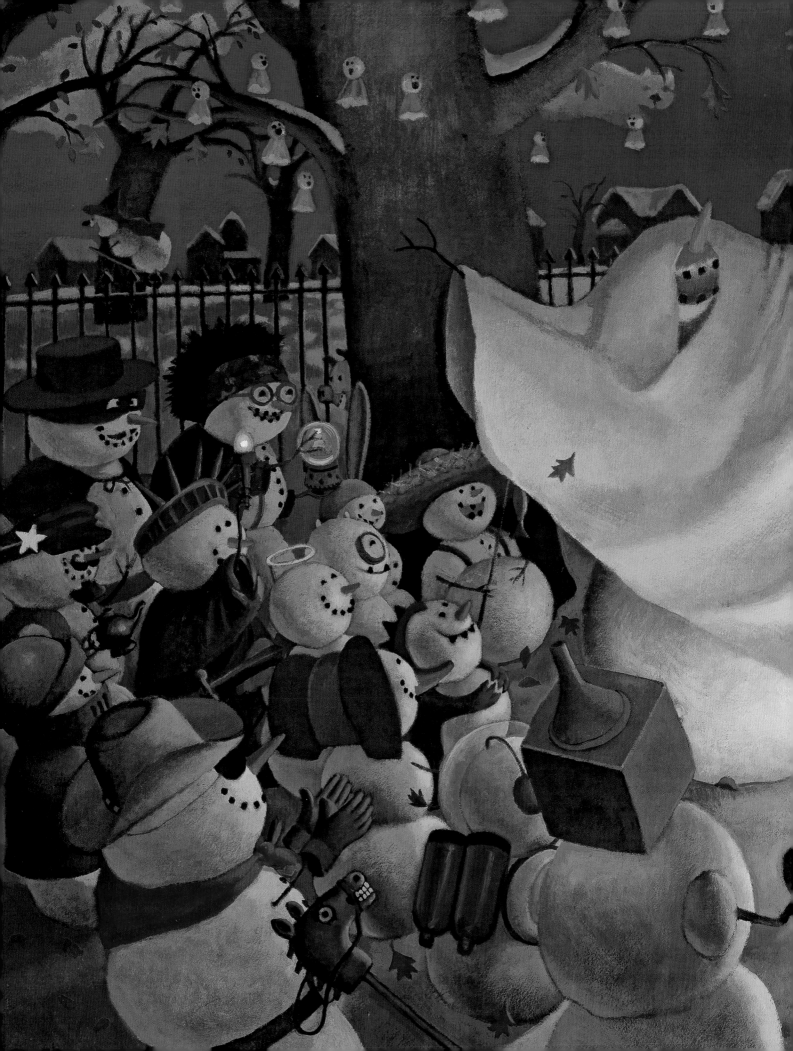

Someone will be telling tales about a snowman ghost.
I'll bet spooky stories is what snowmen like the most!

If their Halloween's like mine, they'll want to trick-or-treat,
And head home with their buckets full of every kind of sweet.

There'll be a lot of giggling on their way back home from town, And it'll take a while before those snowmen settle down.

That's what I thought they'd do, but I guess I'll never know,
Because it warmed up overnight and melted down the snow.

The dress-ups are in piles, but there's something in between—
A snowman message just for us—

"HAPPY HALLOWEEN!"

To Kenzie,
who loves Halloween!

Dial Books for Young Readers
An imprint of Penguin Random House LLC, New York

Text copyright © 2019 by Caralyn Buehner
Pictures copyright © 2019 by Mark Buehner

Visit us online at penguinrandomhouse.com

Printed in China
ISBN 9780525554684

Design by Cerise Steel
Text set in ITC Korinna